I can help like
Super Helping Hero b

MOURNING CLOAK/PHOTOGRAPH BY PETER AND SANDY GREGG/IMAGERY

name   date

Super Helping Hero

A BOOK ABOUT HELPFULNESS

Barbra Minar
Illustrated by Paul Harvey

Chariot Books™
David C. Cook Publishing Co.

Chariot Books™ is an imprint of David C. Cook Publishing Co.
David C. Cook Publishing Co., Elgin, Illinois 60120
David C. Cook Publishing Co., Weston, Ontario
SUPER HELPING HERO
© 1990 David C. Cook Publishing Co., Elgin, IL
All rights reserved.
First Printing, 1990. Printed in the United States of America
94 93 92 91 90 5 4 3 2 1
ISBN 1-55513-960-4 LC 89-60102

The verse marked (TLB) is taken from *The Living Bible* ©1971, owned by assignment by Illir
Regional Bank N.A. (as trustee). Used by permission of Tyndale House Publishers Inc.,
Wheaton, IL 60189. All rights reserved.

Julie Ann put on her red cape. She was playing
JPER HELPING HERO!

Her mother said, "Julie Ann, please help me. Take
is chocolate pie to Mrs. Miller."

"OK," said Julie Ann.

Then Julie Ann thought, *What if I get there and Mrs. Miller's house is on fire? I'll save Mrs. Miller! That's what! I'll be SUPER HELPING HERO!*

But everything at Mrs. Miller's was just fine.
"Oh, thank you, Julie Ann," said Mrs. Miller.
"Could you take these apples next door to Mr. Perry?
It would really help me."
"OK," said Julie Ann.

Then Julie Ann thought, *What if I get there and a big yellow lion is growling at Mr. Perry's door? I'll save Mr. Perry! That's what! I'll be SUPER HELPING HERO!*

But everything at Mr. Perry's was just fine.

"Oh, thank you, Julie Ann," said Mr. Perry.
"Could you take this book next door to Mrs. White? It
would really help me."

"OK," said Julie Ann.

Then Julie Ann thought, *What if I get there and a raging river is flooding Mrs. White's house? I'll save Mrs. White! That's what!* I'll be SUPER HELPING HERO!

But everything at Mrs. White's was just fine.

"Oh, thank you, Julie Ann," said Mrs. White. "Could you take Tommy home to play with your little brother? It would really help me."

"Sure," said Julie Ann.

Then Julie Ann thought, *What if a ferocious orange tiger is growling at my little brother? I'll save him! That's what! I'll be SUPER HELPING HERO!*

But when she got home, everything was fine. Julie Ann felt sad.

"What's the matter?" asked Mother.

"I wanted to be SUPER HELPING HERO, but I only

      took a pie to Mrs. Miller,

         took apples to Mr. Perry,

            took a book to Mrs. White, and

               took Tommy to our house."

Then Julie Ann thought. She straightened her red cape and grinned. "Why, I *am* SUPER HELPING HERO!"

"That's right," Mother said. "When you help others, it's like helping Jesus. It makes Him very happy—and it makes me happy, too. I love my SUPER HELPING HERO." And she gave Julie Ann a big hug.